The Night Before Christmas

by Clement Clarke Moore

Illustrated by Tasha Tudor

Little, Brown and Company
Boston   New York   London

'Twas the night before Christmas,
When all through the house

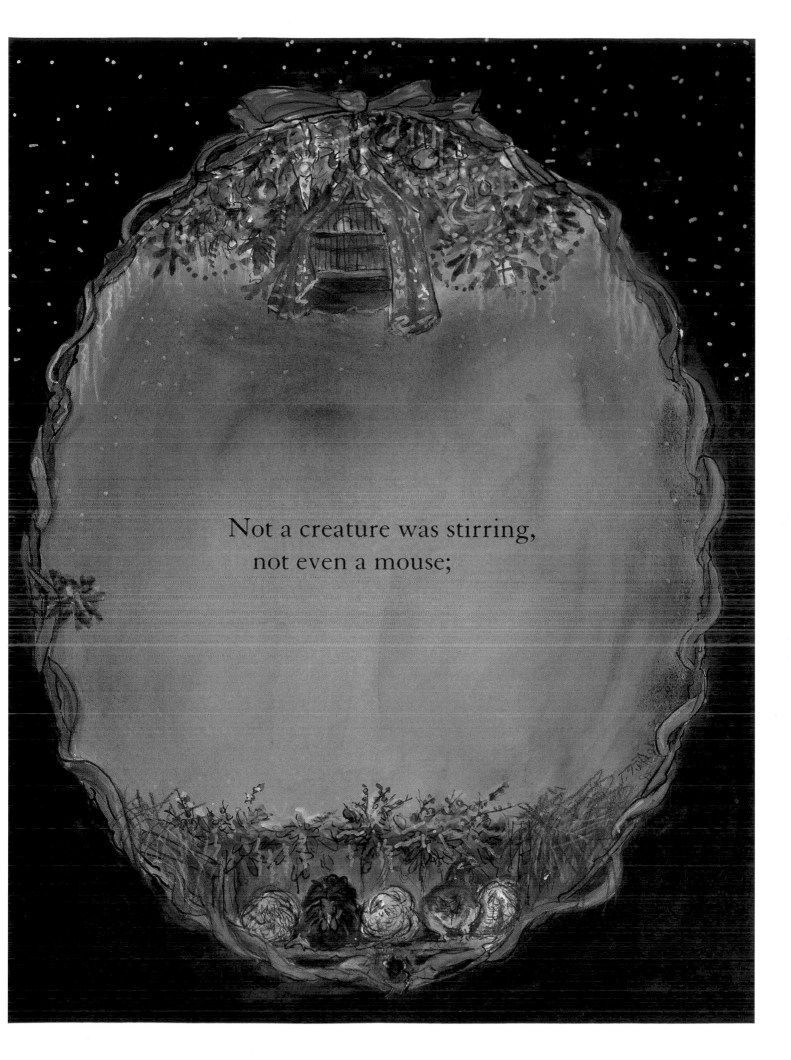

Not a creature was stirring,
not even a mouse;

The stockings were hung
by the chimney with care,
In the hopes that Saint Nicholas
soon would be there;

The children were nestled
all snug in their beds,
While visions of sugarplums
danced in their heads;

And Mama in her kerchief
and I in my cap
Had just settled down
for a long winter's nap,

When out on the lawn
there arose such a clatter,
I sprang from my bed
to see what was the matter.
Away to the window
I flew like a flash,
Tore open the shutters
and threw up the sash.

The moon on the breast
of the new-fallen snow
Gave the lustre of midday
to objects below,
When, what to my wondering
eyes should appear,
But a miniature sleigh
and eight tiny reindeer,
With a little old driver,
so lively and quick,
I knew in a moment
it must be Saint Nick.

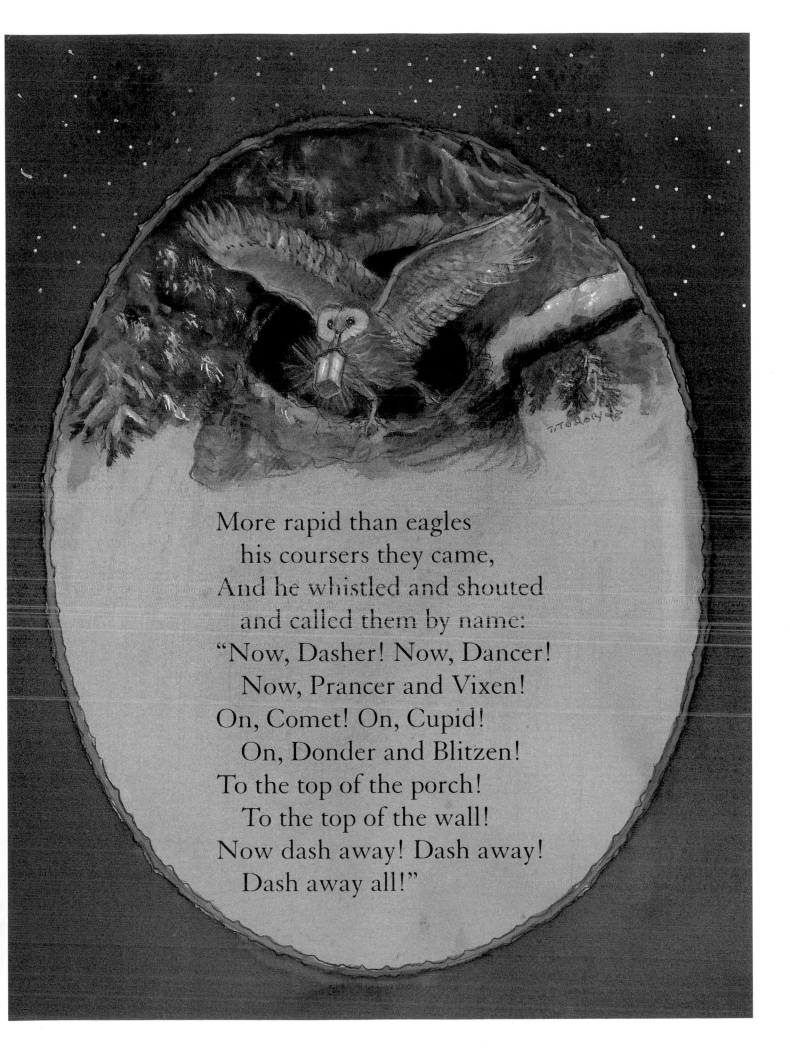

More rapid than eagles
   his coursers they came,
And he whistled and shouted
   and called them by name:
"Now, Dasher! Now, Dancer!
   Now, Prancer and Vixen!
On, Comet! On, Cupid!
   On, Donder and Blitzen!
To the top of the porch!
   To the top of the wall!
Now dash away! Dash away!
   Dash away all!"

As dry leaves that before
    the wild hurricane fly,
When they meet with an obstacle,
    mount to the sky;
So up to the housetop
    the coursers they flew,
With the sleigh full of toys,
    and Saint Nicholas, too.

And then, in a twinkling,
   I heard on the roof
The prancing and pawing
   of each little hoof.
As I drew in my head,
   and was turning around,
Down the chimney Saint Nicholas
   came with a bound.

He was dressed all in fur,
  from his head to his foot,
And his clothes were all tarnished
  with ashes and soot;
A bundle of toys
  he had slung on his back,
And he looked like a peddler
  just opening his pack.
His eyes — how they twinkled!
  His dimples, how merry!
His cheeks were like roses,
  his nose like a cherry!

His droll little mouth
    was drawn up like a bow,
And the beard on his chin
    was as white as the snow;
The stump of a pipe
    he held tight in his teeth,
And the smoke, it encircled
    his head like a wreath.
He had a broad face
    and a little round belly,
That shook when he laughed
    like a bowlful of jelly.

He was chubby and plump,
  a right jolly old elf,
And I laughed when I saw him,
  in spite of myself;
A wink of his eye
  and a twist of his head
Soon gave me to know
  I had nothing to dread.

He spoke not a word
   but went straight to his work,
And filled all the stockings;
   then turned with a jerk,
And laying a finger
   aside of his nose,
And giving a nod,
   up the chimney he rose;

He sprang to his sleigh,
   to his team gave a whistle,
And away they all flew
   like the down of a thistle.
But I heard him exclaim,
   ere he drove out of sight,
"Happy Christmas to all,
   and to all a good night!"

Also by Tasha Tudor:

Corgiville Fair

The Great Corgiville Kidnapping

The Tasha Tudor Cookbook

The Private World of Tasha Tudor

Illustrations copyright © 1999 by Tasha Tudor

First Paperback Edition

Library of Congress Cataloging-in-Publication Data

Moore, Clement Clarke, 1779–1863.
    The night before Christmas / by Clement Clarke Moore ; illustrated by Tasha Tudor.
  — 1st ed.
        p.   cm.
    Summary: Presents the well-known poem about an important Christmas visitor.
    ISBN 0-316-85579-0 (hc) / ISBN 0-316-83271-5 (pb)
    1. Santa Claus — Juvenile poetry.   2. Christmas — Juvenile poetry.
    3. Children's poetry, American.   [1. Santa Claus — Poetry.   2. Christmas — Poetry.
    3. American poetry.   4. Narrative poetry.]   I. Tudor, Tasha, ill.   II. Title.
    PS2429.M5N5   1999b
    811'.2 — dc21   98-21623

                            10 9 8 7 6 5 (hc)
                        10 9 8 7 6 5 4 3 2 1 (pb)

                                    SC

Printed in Hong Kong

The paintings for this book were done in watercolor.
The text was set in Granjon, and the display type is DucDeBerry.